AUG 1 7 '67

Y0-ARD-973

AWN

THE
FOLLETT
BEGINNING-TO-READ
SERIES

Grandmother Dear

Celentha Finfer
Esther Wasserberg
Florence Weinberg

Illustrated by Roy Mathews

Chicago   Follett Publishing Company   New York

Copyright © 1966, by Follett Publishing Company. All rights
reserved. No part of this book may be reproduced in any form
without written permission from the publisher. Manufactured
in the United States of America. Published simultaneously in
Canada by The Ryerson Press, Toronto.

Library of Congress Catalog Card Number: 66-13712

First printing

T/L/A 3455

CO. SCHOOLS
C662750

Grandmother Dear

Is here today.

Please try to help her

While I am away.

I will help Grandma Dear

As much as I can.

You will see, I will be

A good little man.

Now what would you like

To do today?

Read or paint

Or go out to play?

Out to play!

I like that best.

I can play

And you can rest.

I want to ride!

I want to slide!

I want to swing!

I want to hide!

Won't you ride

And slide with me?

Won't you swing

And hide from me?

I cannot ride.

I cannot slide.

I cannot swing.

But I can hide!

Swing up! Swing up!

Oh so high!

Swing down! Swing down!

Please Grandma, try!

Up! Up! Up!

Just like you!

Down! Down! Down!

I'm swinging too!

Away we go now

One, two, three!

This is fun!

Hold on to me!

Come up! Come up!

And then let go.

So fast at first,

And then so slow!

Oh dear me!

It is after three!

Mother is waiting,

For you and me.

Let us skate

Before we go.

Grandmother Dear,

Please don't say "No!"

No! No! No!

Not that! Not that!

I am much too old!

I am much too fat!

You are not too old.

You are not too fat.

Put your right foot front.

Put your left foot back.

Right foot, left foot

See me go!

This IS fun!

You told me so!

Right foot, left foot,

See! Oh see!

My skates are running

Away with me!

No more rides!

No more slides!

No time for more.

It must be four!

Oh Mother, Mother,

You should see

The games that Grandma

Played with me!

You told me to help her,

And I tried.

I helped Grandma skate!

I helped Grandma slide!

Grandmother played?

Oh, yes! I had fun!

I liked every game.

I liked every one!

CO. SCHOOLS
C662750

But now I must rest.

I will rest right here.

ZZZ - ZZZZZZZ - ZZ

Went Grandmother Dear!

GRANDMOTHER DEAR

Reading Level: Level One. *Grandmother Dear* has a total vocabulary of 111 words. It has been tested in first grade classes, where it was read with ease.

Uses of this Book: Reading for fun. Grandmother Dear comes to spend the day and has quite a busy time. Children will enjoy all the funny things Grandma does.

Word List

All of the 111 words used in *Grandmother Dear* are listed. Regular possessives and contractions *(-'s, -n't, -'ll, -'m)* and regular verb forms *(-s, -ed, -ing)* of words already on the list are not listed separately, but the endings are given in parentheses after the word.

5 Grandmother	as	or
Dear	much	paint
is	can	go
here	you	out
today	see	play (ed)
please	be	**8** that
try	a	best
to	good	and
help (ed)	little	rest
her	man	**9** want
while	**7** now	ride (s)
I ('m)	what	slide (s)
am	would	swing (ing)
away	like (ed)	hide
6 will	do (n't)	**10** won't
Grandma	read	with

me
from
11 cannot
but
12 up
oh
so
high
down
13 just
too
14 we
one
two
three
this
fun
hold
on
16 come
then

let
fast
at
first
slow
17 it
after
Mother
waiting
for
18 us
skate (s)
before
say
no
19 not
old
fat
20 are
put
your

right
foot
front
left
back
21 told
22 my
running
24 more
time
must
four
25 should
the
game (s)
26 tried
27 yes
had
every
28 must
went

The Follett BEGINNING-TO-READ Books

Purpose of the Beginning-to-Read Books: To provide easy-to-read materials that will appeal to the interests of primary children. Careful attention is given to vocabulary load and sentence length, but the first criterion is interest to children.

Reading Levels: These books are written at three reading levels, indicated by one, two, or three dots beneath the *Beginning-to-Read* symbol on the back cover. *Level One* books can be read by first grade children in the last half of the school year. As children increase their reading ability they will be able to enjoy *Level Two* books. And as they grow further in their reading ability they will progress to *Level Three* books. Some first grade children will read *Level Two* and *Level Three* books. Many third graders, and even some fourth graders, will read and enjoy *Level One* and *Level Two* books, as well as *Level Three* books. The range of interest of *Beginning-to-Read* books stretches far beyond their reading level.

Use of the Beginning-to-Read Books: Because of their high interest and readability, these books are ideal for independent reading by primary children—at school, in the library, and at home. The books may also be incorporated into the basic reading program to develop children's interests, expand their vocabularies, and improve word-attack skills. It has been suggested that they might serve as the foundation for a skillfully directed reading program. Many *Beginning-to-Read* books correlate with the social studies, science, and other subject fields. All will help children grow in the language arts. Children will read the *Beginning-to-Read* books with confidence, with success, and with real enjoyment.